The Power Couple

Matthew Gage

Published by MG Books, 2025.

THE POWER COUPLE

First edition. March 19, 2025.

Copyright © 2025 Matthew Gage.

ISBN: 979-8230695325

Written by Matthew Gage.

Table of Contents

Chapter 1

The neon glow of Times Square cast an electric hue over the rain-slicked streets of New York City as Maxwell 'Max' Johnson stepped out onto the pavement. His heart pounded in his chest, a rhythmic thrum that echoed the city's relentless pulse. Tonight was the night. His first patrol as a superhero. The weight of his new responsibilities settled on his broad shoulders, but it was a burden he embraced with a mix of excitement and trepidation. The sleek black and gold suit hugged his muscular frame, the golden emblem on his chest gleaming under the artificial light. His short afro was damp from the evening drizzle, and his glowing gold eyes scanned the bustling crowd, searching for any sign of trouble.

Max had always been the skinny, bespectacled nerd, obsessed with comic books and science. But that was before the radioactive hamburger. Before the accident that had transformed him into something more. Now, he was invincible, fast, strong—a force to be reckoned with. Yet, despite his newfound powers, he still felt like that awkward kid deep down, unsure of himself in social situations, overthinking every word and gesture. But tonight, he wasn't Max the nerd. Tonight, he was the protector of New York City.

He took to the skies, his supersonic flight cutting through the cool night air. The city sprawled beneath him like a living, breathing organism, its lights a tapestry of stories and lives. He soared over Central Park, its lush greenery a stark contrast to the concrete jungle, and glided past the towering Empire State Building, its spire piercing the clouds. His senses were heightened, every sound and scent amplified. He could hear the distant laughter of a couple walking their dog, the hum of traffic on the FDR Drive, and the faint strains of jazz drifting from a rooftop bar.

But amidst the symphony of the city, one sound stood out—the shrill wail of an alarm. Max's head snapped toward the source, his instincts kicking in. A bank robbery. Downtown, near Wall Street. He pushed himself faster, his body a blur as he descended toward the scene.

The bank was a modern glass-and-steel structure, its sleek design now marred by the chaos unfolding inside. Max landed with a thud on the wet pavement, his cape billowing behind him like a dark shadow. The alarm blared, its piercing sound echoing through the night. He took a deep breath, his glowing eyes narrowing as he assessed the situation. Inside, masked robbers were shouting, their voices laced with panic and aggression. Guns were pointed at terrified civilians, their faces pale and trembling.

Without hesitation, Max burst through the glass doors, the shattering fragments raining down around him. The robbers froze, their eyes widening at the sight of the towering figure in the black and gold suit. His presence was commanding, his stance confident despite the nerves churning in his stomach. This was it. His first real test.

"Drop your weapons," Max's voice boomed, deep and authoritative. His words cut through the chaos like a knife. The robbers hesitated, their fingers tightening around their guns. Max didn't wait. He moved with a speed that defied comprehension, his enhanced agility allowing him to close the distance in an instant. He disarmed the first robber with a swift kick, the gun flying from the man's hand and skidding across the floor. The second robber fired, but Max caught the bullet mid-air, his invincibility rendering the attack useless. He crushed the bullet between his fingers and tossed it aside before grabbing the robber by the collar and slamming him into the wall.

The remaining robbers tried to flee, but Max was everywhere at once. He blocked their path, his strength overwhelming as he subdued them one by one. Within minutes, the robbery was over. The civilians were safe, their relief palpable as they huddled together, whispering in awe of the hero who had saved them.

Max stood in the center of the bank, his chest rising and falling as he caught his breath. His heart was still racing, but it was a different kind of adrenaline now—the satisfaction of a job well done. He turned to the civilians, his glowing eyes softening as he offered them a reassuring smile. "You're safe now. The police will be here shortly."

As he spoke, a voice called out from behind him. "Hey, nice work."

Max turned, his gaze falling on a woman standing in the doorway. She was stunning, her presence commanding attention even in the aftermath of chaos. Her raven-black hair was pulled into a high ponytail, accentuating her sharp features. Her deep brown eyes sparkled with admiration, and a small scar above her left eyebrow added a touch of rugged charm. She wore a sleek red and white leotard with knee-high boots and a long skirt with a high slit, her costume form-fitting and practical yet elegant.

Max felt his heart skip a beat. She was beautiful, and for a moment, he forgot where he was. His mind went blank, his usual awkwardness threatening to resurface. But he forced himself to respond, trying to sound casual despite the racing thoughts in his head. "Thanks," he replied, his voice steady.

She smiled, her expression warm and infectious. "You're new here, aren't you?"

Max nodded, feeling a flush creep up his neck. "Yeah, first day on the job."

She laughed softly, her laughter like music. "Me too. Just moved to the city. Guess we're both figuring things out."

Max grinned, charmed by her easy demeanor. "Guess so. I'm Max, by the way."

"Kira," she said, extending her hand.

He shook it, her touch sending a jolt through him. Her grip was firm, confident, and he felt a connection—a spark that he couldn't quite explain. "Well, Max, looks like you've got this under control. I'll see you around."

She winked and turned to leave, her confident stride leaving Max staring after her. "Bye," he called out, his voice slightly hoarse. As he watched her disappear into the night, he couldn't help but feel a pang of longing. Despite his newfound powers and the city's admiration, he was still the same skinny nerd deep down, unsure of himself in the face of someone as captivating as Kira.

The police arrived shortly after, their sirens wailing as they took over the scene. Max lingered for a moment, watching as the officers secured the robbers and comforted the civilians. He knew his work here was done, but he couldn't shake the feeling that this was just the beginning. The city needed him, and he was ready to answer the call.

But as he took to the skies once more, his thoughts kept drifting back to Kira. She was new in town, just like him. A fellow hero, perhaps? The idea was intriguing, and he found himself hoping their paths would cross again. Yet, he couldn't shake the doubt that crept into his mind. Someone like her—confident, beautiful, disciplined—would never notice someone like him. Not the awkward nerd he still felt like inside.

He sighed, the cool night air whipping past him as he soared over the city. For now, he had a job to do. A city to protect. And a heart to keep in check. But as he flew, the neon lights of New York City twinkling below, he couldn't help but wonder what the future held. Would he see Kira again? Would he ever find the courage to truly step out of his old self and embrace the hero he was becoming?

The questions lingered, unanswered, as Max continued his patrol, the city's pulse beating in time with his own. The night was young, and the possibilities were endless. For now, he would focus on the task at hand, saving lives and making a difference. But deep down, he knew that the real challenge—the one that truly mattered—was finding his place in this new world. And maybe, just maybe, finding someone to share it with.

The city stretched out before him, a canvas of light and life, and Max felt a sense of purpose he had never known before. He was no longer just Max the nerd. He was a hero. And tonight was only the beginning.

Chapter 2

The night air was crisp, carrying the faint hum of New York City's relentless energy. Kira Yamamoto stood in the dimly lit alleyway, her breath coming in ragged gasps as Animal's iron grip tightened around her throat. The villain's laughter echoed like a mockery, his massive frame towering over her. Kira's regenerative abilities were strained, her body struggling to keep up with the relentless pressure. Her vision blurred at the edges, and for a moment, she thought this might be the end.

Animal's voice was a low growl, dripping with malice. "You're nothing but a bug, samurai girl. Squashing you will be a pleasure."

Kira's fingers clawed at his arm, her blade lying uselessly on the ground a few feet away. She could feel her strength waning, her healing powers barely keeping her conscious. Just as Animal's grip tightened further, a thunderous crash shook the alley. The ground trembled, and Kira's head snapped up, her eyes widening in surprise.

A figure burst through the brick wall at the end of the alley, sending debris flying. Max stood there, his towering frame radiating raw power. His black and gold suit gleamed under the flickering streetlight, and his glowing gold eyes locked onto Animal with an intensity that made even the villain hesitate.

"Let her go," Max growled, his voice deep and commanding.

Animal's lips curled into a sneer. "And who's going to make me, pretty boy? You?"

Without another word, Max charged. The air seemed to crackle with energy as he moved, his speed a blur. Animal dropped Kira, who crumpled to the ground, gasping for air. She watched in stunned silence as Max and Animal collided, their clash shaking the alley like an earthquake.

Max's strength was undeniable. He slammed Animal into a nearby dumpster, denting the metal with a deafening clang. But Animal was no pushover; he roared, his animalistic strength surging as he countered with a blow that sent Max staggering back. Kira pushed herself up, her throat still throbbing, and grabbed her blade, ready to rejoin the fight.

Before she could move, Max launched himself at Animal again, this time using his invincibility to absorb the villain's attacks. With a final, earth-shattering blow, Max sent Animal flying across the alley. The villain crashed into a stack of crates, which splintered under his weight, leaving him dazed and motionless.

Kira took a shaky breath, her hand clutching her throat. She pushed herself to her feet, her blade still gripped tightly in her other hand. Max turned to her, his expression unreadable beneath his mask.

"You okay?" he asked, his voice steady but concerned.

Kira managed a weak smile. "Thanks. I had him on the ropes..."

Max chuckled, the sound deep and rumbling. "I'm sure you did."

She extended a hand, her tone turning serious. "Want to team up? I could use someone... super strong on my side."

Max hesitated, his gaze dropping to the ground. "I'm used to working alone," he admitted awkwardly.

Kira nodded, understanding flashing in her eyes. "Me too. But maybe we're stronger together."

He considered her words, then nodded. "Alright."

The alley fell silent for a moment, the only sound the distant hum of the city. Kira sheathed her blade and straightened her leotard, her movements deliberate. "We should get out of here before the cops show up," she said, gesturing toward the street.

Max followed her lead, his steps heavy but purposeful. As they walked through the city, the silence stretched between them until Kira broke it. "You're quiet," she observed, glancing at him.

Max shrugged, a faint blush creeping up his neck. "This is the longest conversation I've ever had with a girl besides my mom."

Kira laughed, a genuine sound that eased the tension. "For a muscular hulk like you, I'd think you'd be talking to women all the time."

He shook his head, a hint of a smile playing on his lips. "I was a skinny nerd before all this."

She nodded, her curiosity piqued. "What's your power, then?"

Max explained his abilities, his voice steady but guarded. "Super strength, invincibility, speed, agility, and flight. Got them after... an accident with a radioactive hamburger."

Kira raised an eyebrow, a smile tugging at her lips. "A hamburger? That's... unique."

He chuckled, a hint of self-deprecation in his tone. "Yeah, well, it's not every day you get superpowers from fast food."

"Impressive," Kira said, her tone admiring. "I've got renegotiated health and a blade—been training my whole life."

Max raised an eyebrow. "It shows. You're skilled."

She winked, playing it off. "Lifetime of practice."

They walked in comfortable silence for a while, the city lights casting long shadows around them. Eventually, they reached a street where Kira's motorcycle was parked. She swung her leg over the seat, her hand resting on the throttle.

"It's been nice talking to you," she said, her tone warm. "See you around."

Max hesitated, then called out, "Wait—how will I call you?"

Kira smiled, and grabbed a pen that was in a pouch on her motorcycle. She then grabbed his hand, and scribbled her number on his palm. "See you around," she grinned, hopping back on her bike, revving the engine before speeding off into the night, leaving Max standing there, a small smile tugging at his lips.

As Kira disappeared into the city's glow, Max couldn't help but feel a strange sense of excitement. Teaming up with someone like her—strong, skilled, and confident—was uncharted territory for him. But there was something about her that made him want to try.

He glanced down at the number on his palm, a faint warmth spreading through his chest. Maybe, just maybe, this was the start of something new.

The city bustled around him, its energy infectious. Max took a deep breath, his glowing gold eyes scanning the horizon. Whatever came next, he was ready.

Meanwhile, Kira weaved through traffic on her motorcycle, the wind whipping through her ponytail. She couldn't shake the feeling that Max was more than just a temporary ally. There was something about him—his awkwardness, his strength, his hidden depth—that intrigued her.

As she reached her apartment, she parked her bike and climbed the stairs, her mind racing. Teaming up with Max felt right, but it also felt... different. She wasn't used to relying on others, but there was something about him that made her want to try.

Inside her apartment, Kira leaned against the door, her blade still sheathed at her side. She closed her eyes, the events of the night replaying in her mind. Max's arrival, his strength, his quiet confidence—it all felt like the beginning of something bigger.

She opened her eyes, a determined glint in her brown irises. Whatever challenges lay ahead, she knew one thing for certain: with Max by her side, she wasn't alone anymore.

The city outside her window continued its relentless hum, a reminder that the world never stopped turning. But for now, Kira allowed herself a moment of stillness, a rare pause in her otherwise chaotic life.

As she turned to face the night, a small smile played on her lips. The future was uncertain, but for the first time in a long while, she felt a spark of hope.

And somewhere out there, Max Johnson felt it too.

Chapter 3

The ground heaved and cracked beneath Max's boots, the tremors sending shards of glass and debris raining down like deadly confetti. The once-bustling streets of downtown Manhattan had transformed into a chaotic nightmare, civilians screaming as they scrambled for safety. Tremor, the villain whose very name struck fear into the hearts of New Yorkers, stood atop a crumbling skyscraper, his arms outstretched as if conducting an orchestra of destruction. His eyes glowed an eerie green, and with each pulse of his power, the earth groaned in response. Max clenched his fists, his golden eyes scanning the chaos. He could feel the weight of every life in danger, every heartbeat racing in fear. But Tremor's relentless assault left him no choice—he couldn't save them all if he didn't stop the source of the chaos first.

With a deep breath, Max launched himself into the air, his supersonic flight cutting through the smoke-filled sky. Tremor smirked, sensing his approach, and slammed a fist into the ground. The shockwave hit Max like a freight train, sending him careening into the side of a building. The impact barely fazed him, but it was enough to slow him down. As he pushed himself back into the air, his mind raced. He needed help. He couldn't do this alone.

His fingers flew to his comms device, and with a quick tap, he dialed Kira's number. The line connected instantly, her voice calm and steady despite the urgency in his tone.

"Kira, it's Max. I need you. Tremor's here, and I can't—"

"On my way," she interrupted, her voice cutting through the chaos like a blade.

Max didn't waste time explaining further. He knew Kira would understand. She always did.

Minutes felt like hours as Max fought to contain the damage, his strength and speed pushing him to the limit. He lifted a collapsing building just long enough for a group of civilians to escape, his muscles straining under the weight. But as soon as he set it down, Tremor struck again, the ground splitting open and swallowing the structure whole. Max's heart sank as screams echoed through the air. He couldn't be everywhere at once.

Then, like a crimson and white comet, Kira descended from the sky. Her sword was drawn, her movements graceful yet deadly as she landed between Max and Tremor. Her brown eyes locked onto the villain, her expression unyielding.

"Max," she called out, her voice cutting through the noise. "Focus on the civilians. I'll handle him."

Max nodded, gratitude flashing in his eyes before he turned his attention back to the chaos. Kira's presence was a balm to his frayed nerves, her confidence a reminder that they were a team. With her taking the lead, he could finally breathe.

Kira advanced on Tremor, her steps deliberate, her sword held at the ready. Tremor laughed, a deep, rumbling sound that seemed to shake the ground itself. "Another hero? You're just in time to watch your city crumble."

"Your reign ends today," Kira replied, her voice cold. "Max, now!"

Max didn't hesitate. With Kira engaging Tremor, he dove into the heart of the destruction, his enhanced speed allowing him to move faster than the falling debris. He caught a woman just as a chunk of concrete careened toward her, lifting her to safety before turning his attention to a group of children trapped in a collapsed bus. His hands worked quickly, tearing through the metal like paper, his strength a lifeline for those inside.

But for every life he saved, another seemed to slip through his fingers. The ground continued to shift and crack, buildings toppling like dominoes. Max's heart pounded in his chest, his mind racing as he tried to prioritize. He couldn't be everywhere at once. He couldn't save everyone.

Kira's battle with Tremor raged on, her sword clashing against his earth-manipulating powers. She moved with precision, her regenerative abilities allowing her to shrug off the minor injuries that would incapacitate a normal person. But Tremor was relentless, his attacks growing stronger with each passing moment.

Max's comms crackled to life, Kira's voice urgent. "Max, I need you to clear the area. I'm going to try something risky."

Max didn't question her. He knew Kira well enough to trust her instincts. He redoubled his efforts, herding civilians to safety as quickly as he could. The ground beneath him trembled violently, but he pushed through the pain, his focus unwavering.

Then, with a final, decisive strike, Kira unleashed a barrage of attacks that left Tremor reeling. She leaped back, her sword glowing with an otherworldly light as she channeled her energy into one final blow. The air crackled with power, and for a moment, time seemed to stand still.

Tremor roared, his body convulsing as Kira's attack hit its mark. The ground stilled, the tremors ceasing as he collapsed to his knees, defeated. Kira stood over him, her chest heaving, her sword pointed at his chest.

"It's over," she said, her voice steady.

Max approached cautiously, his eyes scanning the area for any remaining threats. The silence that followed was deafening, the only sound the distant wail of sirens and the cries of the injured. He saw her then, a woman lying motionless on the ground, her lifeless eyes staring up at the sky. Max's heart sank as he realized he'd been too late. He'd failed her.

Kira sensed his anguish, her sharp eyes catching the direction of his gaze. She sheathed her sword and walked over to him, placing a hand on his shoulder. "Max," she said softly, her voice a mix of compassion and firmness. "You can't save everyone."

Max's eyes met hers, his expression haunted. "I have to try," he replied, his voice breaking. "If I don't, who will?"

Kira pulled him into a tight hug, her strength a reminder that even heroes needed support. "You're not alone in this," she whispered. "We're a team. And sometimes, even heroes need a hug."

Max closed his eyes, letting the weight of the moment wash over him. "Thanks for being here," he murmured, his voice thick with emotion.

Kira smiled, her grin a beacon of hope in the chaos. "Anytime," she said, her voice warm. "That's what partners are for."

As they stood there, surrounded by the ruins of what was once a thriving city, Max felt a sense of resolve settle over him. The battle was over, but the fight was far from finished. Together, they would rebuild, they would protect, and they would never stop trying. Because that was what heroes did.

The sun began to set, casting a golden glow over the wreckage. Max and Kira exchanged a look, unspoken words passing between them. They had a city to save, and they would do it together. Hand in hand, they walked toward the horizon, ready to face whatever challenges lay ahead. The end was nowhere in sight, but with Kira by his side, Max knew they could weather any storm.

Chapter 4

The sun dipped lower in the sky, casting a golden hue over the New York City skyline as Max and Kira lounged on the rooftop, a spread of tacos between them. The air was warm, carrying the faint hum of the city below—car horns, distant laughter, and the rhythmic thrum of life. Max tore into a taco, savoring the combination of crispy shell and savory filling, while Kira leaned back on her elbows, her gaze fixed on the towering skyscrapers that seemed to touch the clouds.

"Amazing view," Kira murmured, her voice soft but carrying a weight of appreciation.

Max nodded, his mouth full. "Yeah, it really is." He swallowed, wiping a bit of salsa from his chin with the back of his hand. "Sometimes I forget how beautiful this city can be, especially after a long night of... you know."

Kira smiled faintly, her brown eyes glinting in the sunlight. "Saving the day? Yeah, it's easy to get caught up in the chaos. But moments like this... they remind you why it's worth it."

They fell into a comfortable silence, the kind that only comes between people who've faced life-or-death situations together. Max leaned back, his arms crossed behind his head, and let out a contented sigh. The tacos were good, the company was better, and for once, the city felt still—a rare moment of peace in their otherwise chaotic lives.

"So," Kira said after a while, breaking the silence, "what's it like? Being a hero, I mean. All the attention."

Max shrugged, a hint of awkwardness creeping into his voice. "It's weird, honestly. Before, I couldn't get a date to save my life. Now, suddenly, everyone wants a piece of me." He chuckled, but there was a bitterness beneath the humor. "It's like they only see the suit, not the guy inside it."

Kira raised an eyebrow, her expression curious. "Have you... you know, taken advantage of that?"

Max shook his head, a faint blush creeping up his cheeks. "Nah, not my style. I'm waiting for the right person." He paused, his gaze meeting hers for a moment before he looked away. "Someone who sees me for me, not just the hero."

The air between them seemed to thicken, charged with unspoken words and unacknowledged feelings. Kira stretched, her movements fluid and graceful, her long raven hair cascading over her shoulder. "Break's over, I guess," she said, her tone light but her eyes lingering on him.

Max cleared his throat, trying to shake off the tension. "What are you doing later? I could use some training."

Kira smirked, her lips curling into a playful smile. "Think you can keep up?"

They headed back to Kira's loft, a spacious, sunlit space with high ceilings and exposed brick walls. The main room was cluttered with training equipment—a punching bag, a rack of swords, and a mat spread across the floor. Kira moved with purpose, her every action deliberate, as she began to stretch and warm up. Max watched her for a moment, admiring the precision of her movements, before joining in.

"Alright," Kira said, her voice steady, "let's see what you've got. Hand-to-hand, no powers."

Max nodded, rolling his shoulders. "No problem."

They circled each other, their footsteps quiet on the mat. Max struck first, a quick jab aimed at Kira's midsection, but she sidestepped with ease, her body moving like water. She countered with a swift kick, which Max blocked, but the force of it sent him stumbling back. He grinned, his competitive spirit igniting. "Not bad," he said, lunging forward with a combination of punches.

Kira deflected each strike with calculated precision, her movements economical and efficient. She wasn't as physically strong as Max, but her technique was flawless, honed through years of disciplined training. She feinted left, then spun, delivering a roundhouse kick that caught Max off guard. He grunted as he hit the mat, but he was back on his feet in an instant, his gold eyes gleaming with determination.

The fight continued, a dance of strikes and counters, each of them testing the other's limits. Max's strength and speed were formidable, but Kira's skill and strategy kept her one step ahead. Finally, she saw an opening—a momentary lapse in Max's defense—and she seized it. With a swift motion, she swept his legs out from under him and pinned him to the mat, straddling his waist. Her breath came in short gasps, her face inches from his.

"All the power in the world means nothing if you can't control it," she said, her voice steady but her eyes intense.

Max nodded, a mix of frustration and admiration swirling within him. "You're right," he admitted. "I rely too much on my abilities. I need to learn to fight smarter, not just harder."

Kira smirked, her grip on his wrists loosening. "That's the spirit. Now, get up. We're not done yet."

They trained for another hour, Max focusing on technique and precision rather than brute force. By the end, he was drenched in sweat, his muscles aching, but he felt a sense of accomplishment. Kira, ever the disciplined warrior, showed no signs of fatigue, her movements as graceful as ever.

"Want to stay?" she asked casually, wiping her hands on a towel. "Watch a movie or something?"

Max agreed readily, and they settled on the couch, a blanket draped over their legs as the film played on the screen. It was an action movie, full of explosions and heroic feats, but Max found himself more interested in the woman sitting beside him. Her presence was comforting, her strength a quiet reassurance. He wanted to kiss her—the urge was almost overwhelming—but he held back, respecting the unspoken boundary between them.

After the movie ended, they sat in silence for a moment, the credits rolling on the screen. Max turned to Kira, his heart pounding in his chest. "Thanks," he said, his voice soft. "For everything. For today, for... for being my partner."

Kira smiled, her eyes warm. "Anytime, Max. We're a team, remember?"

He nodded, but as he waved goodbye and headed for the door, a bittersweet feeling lingered. He wished they were more than just partners, but for now, this was enough. As he stepped out into the bustling streets of New York City, he felt a renewed sense of purpose. Together, they would protect this city, no matter the cost. And maybe, just maybe, one day they'd be more than just allies.

The city lights glowed around him, a reminder of the lives they fought to protect. Max took a deep breath, his gold eyes gleaming in the darkness, and smiled. Whatever the future held, he knew one thing for certain: with Kira by his side, he could face anything.

Chapter 5

The evening sun cast a golden hue over New York City, its rays filtering through the floor-to-ceiling windows of Kira's loft. The spacious apartment, adorned with minimalist furniture and a few carefully chosen pieces of Japanese art, felt unusually tense. Max and Kira sat side by side on the leather couch, their usual banter replaced by a heavy silence. The news played on the flat-screen TV mounted on the opposite wall, its volume turned up just enough to fill the room with the somber voice of the newscaster.

Footage of a distant African country dominated the screen. Tanks rolled through dusty streets, their tracks crushing the remnants of what had once been bustling marketplaces. Soldiers in dark green uniforms marched in formation, their faces hardened by war. The camera panned to a village in flames, smoke rising in thick, black plumes. Women and children ran in panic, their cries muffled by the distance but no less chilling. The newscaster's voice cracked as he reported the latest atrocities. "The warlord's forces show no mercy. Entire villages have been wiped out. Women and children are not spared. The international community watches in horror, but no one has stepped in to stop him."

Max's jaw tightened, his fists clenching the cushions of the couch. His gold eyes glowed faintly, a sign of his rising anger. "We can't just sit here and watch this," he muttered, his voice low and tight. "This isn't right, Kira. We have the power to stop this. We have the power."

Kira sighed, her gaze still fixed on the screen. Her hands were folded in her lap, her posture rigid. "Max, we're superheroes, not soldiers. We fight villains, not nations. This isn't our fight."

Max whipped his head to face her, his expression a mix of frustration and disbelief. "They're the villains, Kira. Look at what they're doing! We were given these powers to save people, not hide behind excuses. If we don't act, who will?"

Kira's brow furrowed, her brown eyes meeting his with a steady resolve. "It's not that simple. We're American citizens. If we interfere, it could be seen as an act of war. We could escalate this into something even worse."

"Worse than genocide?" Max shot back, his voice rising. "Worse than watching innocent people die while we do nothing? We're not politicians, Kira. We're heroes. We don't need permission to do what's right."

Kira's shoulders tensed, her frustration mirroring his own. "Max, I get it. I do. But we can't just fly into another country and start throwing punches. There are consequences. We could make things worse."

Max stood abruptly, his tall frame casting a shadow over the couch. "I don't care about the consequences. I can't sit here and do nothing. If you won't come with me, I'll go alone."

He strode toward the window, his black and gold suit gleaming in the fading light. Kira watched him, her heart torn between her sense of duty and her fear of the unknown. She knew Max was right—they had the power to make a difference. But she also knew the risks. The world was watching, and their actions could have far-reaching consequences.

"Wait," she called out, her voice steady despite the turmoil in her chest. She stood, crossing the room to stand beside him. The news continued to play in the background, a grim reminder of the stakes. "I'm your partner, Max. If you're going, I'm going. Damn the consequences."

Max turned to face her, a small smile playing on his lips. Without a word, he grabbed her hand, his grip warm and reassuring. Together, they stepped toward the open window, the cool evening air rushing in to meet them. Kira felt a surge of determination as Max's other hand enveloped hers, his strength a tangible reminder of their bond.

"Ready?" he asked, his voice calm despite the storm in his eyes.

Kira nodded, her heart pounding in her chest. "Let's go."

In a blur of motion, they soared out the window, cutting through the sky like a comet. The city fell away beneath them, its lights twinkling like stars as they ascended. Max's speed was exhilarating, the wind whipping through Kira's hair as they hurtled toward the horizon. She glanced at him, his profile sharp against the backdrop of the setting sun, and felt a surge of gratitude for his unwavering resolve.

The journey was long, but Max's supersonic flight made it seem almost effortless. Hours passed like minutes as they crossed oceans and continents, the world shrinking beneath them. Finally, the war-torn country came into view, its landscape scarred by violence. Smoke rose from burning villages, and the sound of gunfire echoed across the plains.

They landed on the outskirts of a village, the air thick with the smell of smoke and blood. The warlord's army was everywhere, their dark green uniforms a stark contrast to the devastation around them. Max and Kira exchanged a glance, their unspoken agreement clear. They were here to fight, to protect, to make a difference.

Max charged into the fray first, his invincibility and strength making him a force to be reckoned with. He plowed through enemy lines, his fists sending soldiers flying like ragdolls. Kira followed close behind, her agility and precision a deadly combination. She moved like a shadow, her sword slicing through the air with surgical efficiency. Together, they were a whirlwind of destruction, their powers unleashed in a symphony of violence.

The warlord's soldiers were no match for them. Max's strength tore through their ranks, while Kira's blade found its mark with unerring accuracy. The battle was chaotic, the air filled with the screams of the dying and the roar of gunfire. But Max and Kira fought with a purpose, their actions driven by a desire to protect the innocent.

As they fought, Kira caught glimpses of the villagers cowering in fear, their eyes wide with terror. Children clung to their mothers, their faces streaked with tears. Kira's heart ached for them, her resolve hardening with every step. She fought not just for herself, but for them—for the lives that hung in the balance.

The warlord himself emerged from the chaos, a towering figure clad in heavy armor. His face was hidden behind a helmet, his voice a deep, menacing growl. "Who dares challenge me?" he bellowed, his hand resting on the hilt of a massive sword.

Max stepped forward, his gold eyes glowing with determination. "We do," he declared, his voice carrying across the battlefield. "And we're here to stop you."

The warlord laughed, a cruel, mocking sound. "You think you can defeat me? You're fools. My army is unstoppable."

Kira stepped beside Max, her sword held at the ready. "We'll see about that."

The warlord charged, his sword swinging in a wide arc. Max met him head-on, their weapons clashing in a shower of sparks. The warlord was strong, his blows powerful, but Max's invincibility gave him the edge. Kira circled around them, looking for an opening, her movements graceful and calculated.

The battle was fierce, the air thick with tension. Max and the warlord traded blows, their struggle a test of strength and will. Kira watched for her moment, her blade poised to strike. Finally, she saw it—a gap in the warlord's defenses. With a swift, precise movement, she lunged forward, her sword slicing through the air.

The warlord roared in pain as Kira's blade found its mark, his armor no match for her skill. He stumbled back, his sword falling from his grasp. Max seized the opportunity, delivering a final, decisive blow that sent the warlord crashing to the ground.

The battle ended as abruptly as it had begun. The warlord's soldiers, leaderless and demoralized, threw down their weapons and surrendered. The villagers, once cowering in fear, emerged from their hiding places, their faces filled with hope.

"Kira! Max! Thank you!" they cried, their voices a chorus of gratitude. "You saved us!"

Max and Kira stood side by side, their chests heaving with exhaustion. They waved to the crowd, a mix of triumph and relief washing over them. Max leaned close to Kira, his voice barely audible over the cheers. "See? It was worth it."

Kira smiled, her heart swelling with pride. "Definitely."

But as they stood there, basking in the gratitude of the people they had saved, a shadow fell over their victory. The sound of approaching helicopters broke through the cheers, their rotors chopping the air. Max and Kira exchanged a glance, their smiles fading. They knew what was coming.

The helicopters landed on the outskirts of the village, their doors sliding open to reveal a team of armed soldiers. They wore the insignia of the United Nations, their faces stern and unyielding. A man in a crisp suit stepped forward, his voice carrying across the distance.

"Maxwell Johnson and Kira Yamamoto, you are under arrest for violating international law. As American citizens, your actions constitute an act of war. You are to come with us immediately."

Max's jaw tightened, his gold eyes flashing with anger. Kira stood beside him, her sword still in hand, her expression unreadable. They had known the risks, but hearing the words aloud made them all too real.

"We were just trying to help," Max said, his voice steady.

The man in the suit shook his head, his expression grim. "Your intentions do not matter. You have crossed a line, and there will be consequences."

Kira sheathed her sword, her movements slow and deliberate. She knew fighting was not the answer. Not now. Not here. "We'll come quietly," she said, her voice calm. "But know this—we did what we had to do. We saved lives."

Max nodded, his gaze meeting hers. Together, they walked toward the helicopters, their heads held high. The villagers watched in silence, their gratitude mingled with fear. Max and Kira had saved them, but at what cost?

As they boarded the helicopter, Kira glanced back at the village one last time. The smoke was clearing, the cries of the wounded fading into the distance. She knew they had made a difference, but the price they would pay remained to be seen.

The helicopter lifted off, carrying them away from the chaos they had left behind. Max sat beside Kira, his expression unreadable. She reached for his hand, her fingers intertwining with his. He squeezed her hand gently, a silent acknowledgment of their shared burden.

They flew back to New York City in silence, the weight of their actions pressing down on them. The city lights twinkled below, a stark contrast to the devastation they had witnessed. Kira leaned her head against the window, her thoughts a whirlwind of emotions.

"Do you think we did the right thing?" Max asked, his voice soft.

Kira closed her eyes, her heart heavy. "I don't know," she admitted. "But I know we couldn't have done nothing."

Max nodded, his gaze fixed on the horizon. "We'll face whatever comes next together. That's all we can do."

Kira smiled faintly, grateful for his unwavering support. "Together," she agreed.

The helicopter landed on the rooftop of a UN building, its rotors slowing to a stop. Max and Kira stepped out, their hands still clasped, their faces set with determination. They knew the road ahead would be difficult, but they also knew they had each other.

As they were led into the building, Kira glanced at Max, her heart filled with a mix of fear and resolve. Whatever happened next, they would face it together. They were partners, not just in heroism, but in life. And no matter the consequences, they would stand by each other's side.

Chapter 6

The courtroom fell silent as the heavy wooden doors swung open, their hinges groaning under the weight of the moment. A gust of wind swept through the chamber, carrying with it the faint scent of rain and the promise of change. All eyes turned toward the entrance, where a figure stood bathed in the soft morning light streaming through the stained-glass windows. It was not just one figure, but a procession of them, each clad in the vibrant colors and symbols of their respective nations. The international superheroes had arrived.

Leading the group was Valkyrie, a towering woman from Norway, her platinum blonde hair braided intricately and adorned with feathers. Her armor gleamed with the blue, red, and white of the Norwegian flag, and her presence commanded respect. Beside her stood Samurai Rising, a Japanese hero whose crimson and white armor mirrored Kira's own, though his was adorned with the rising sun emblem. His stoic expression betrayed a deep sense of purpose. From France came Éclair, a lithe figure in a blue and white bodysuit, her mask shaped like a lightning bolt, symbolizing the speed and precision of her nation. Guardian Bear, a hulking figure from Russia, wore a suit of fur-lined armor, his bear-like helmet a nod to his country's wildlife and strength. Golden Phoenix, representing China, stood tall in her fiery red and gold attire, her wings spreading slightly as if ready to take flight. And from Brazil, Carnaval, a vibrant hero whose costume shimmered with the colors of the rainforest, brought an air of festivity and resilience.

The group moved with purpose, their capes billowing behind them as they approached the defense table where Max and Kira sat. The courtroom buzzed with whispers, the tension palpable. Judge Eleanor Hargrove, a stern woman in her sixties with silver hair pulled into a tight bun, rapped her gavel sharply. "Order! This court will come to order!"

Valkyrie stepped forward, her voice resonating with authority. "We have come to speak on behalf of Maxwell Johnson and Kira Yamamoto.

Their actions, though unorthodox, were taken in the name of justice and the protection of innocent lives. We stand with them, not as representatives of our nations, but as guardians of humanity."

The gallery erupted in murmurs, the international press scrambling to capture every word. Judge Hargrove raised a hand, her expression unreadable. "This is highly irregular. Who speaks for you, and under what authority?"

Samurai Rising bowed his head slightly, his voice steady. "We speak for the collective conscience of heroes around the world. The boundaries of international law cannot confine the duty we have to protect the vulnerable. Max and Kira acted when no one else would. Their courage should be commended, not condemned."

Éclair stepped forward, her French accent lending a melodic quality to her words. "The world is changing. Threats no longer respect borders, and neither should our response. Max and Kira's actions were a necessary intervention, one that prevented a greater catastrophe."

Guardian Bear's deep voice rumbled through the room. "In Russia, we say, 'A hero is not measured by the laws they follow, but by the lives they save.' Max and Kira are heroes. They deserve our gratitude, not our judgment."

Golden Phoenix spread her arms, her voice filled with passion. "In China, we believe in the balance of yin and yang. Sometimes, to maintain harmony, one must act boldly. Max and Kira restored balance to a land torn apart by chaos. Their actions were just."

Carnaval's smile was warm, but her words carried weight. "In Brazil, we celebrate life and the courage it takes to defend it. Max and Kira fought for life, for hope, for the future. They are heroes, not criminals."

The courtroom was electric, the air thick with the weight of their words. Max and Kira exchanged a glance, a silent acknowledgment of the support they now had. Max's glowing gold eyes met Kira's piercing brown ones, and for a moment, the chaos of the trial faded away. They were not alone.

Judge Hargrove leaned forward, her gaze sweeping over the assembled heroes. "Your words are compelling, but this is a court of law, not a council of heroes. Max and Kira's actions violated international sovereignty. That is undeniable."

Valkyrie's expression hardened. "And yet, it is also undeniable that their actions saved lives. The question before us is not whether they broke the law, but whether the law itself is just in this instance. If the law fails to protect the innocent, then it is the law that must change."

The gallery erupted in applause, quickly silenced by the judge's gavel. Hargrove's eyes narrowed, her voice firm. "This court will recess for one hour while we consider the implications of your statements. Be advised, this is not a precedent we take lightly."

As the judge stood and exited the chamber, the international heroes gathered around Max and Kira. Samurai Rising placed a hand on Max's shoulder. "You did what was right. Never doubt that."

Éclair smiled at Kira. "You fought with honor. The world sees that, even if the law does not."

Max exhaled, his shoulders relaxing slightly. "I appreciate your support, but I can't shake the feeling that we've opened a can of worms here. What happens if every hero starts acting outside the law?"

Golden Phoenix's eyes glinted with determination. "Then perhaps it is time for heroes to unite, to create a new framework that transcends borders. A global alliance, one that can act where governments cannot."

Carnaval's laughter was infectious. "Imagine it—a world where heroes are not bound by politics, but by the simple truth of what is right. It's a beautiful dream, no?"

Kira's expression was thoughtful. "It's a dream worth fighting for. But it won't be easy. The world is complicated, and not everyone will agree with our methods."

Guardian Bear nodded. "Nothing worth doing is ever easy. But together, we can make it happen. The question is, are you ready to lead this charge?"

Max and Kira shared another glance, the weight of the moment settling on their shoulders. Max spoke first, his voice steady. "If it means saving lives and making the world a better place, then yes. We're ready."

Kira's voice was soft but resolute. "We've always fought for what's right. This is just the next step."

As the courtroom emptied for the recess, the international heroes remained, their presence a silent promise of solidarity. Outside, the rain had begun to fall, its gentle patter a soothing contrast to the storm brewing within the walls of the courtroom. The world was watching, and for the first time, it seemed possible that heroes might not just save lives—they might change the world.

The recess was a whirlwind of activity. Reporters swarmed the courthouse steps, their cameras flashing as they sought comments from the international heroes. Valkyrie and Samurai Rising fielded questions with poise, their answers measured but firm. Éclair and Carnaval engaged with the crowd, their charisma winning over even the most skeptical of journalists. Guardian Bear and Golden Phoenix stood as silent sentinels, their mere presence a reminder of the strength and unity of the group.

Inside, Max and Kira sat in a small conference room, their legal team huddled around them. The atmosphere was tense but hopeful. "This is unprecedented," said their lawyer, a sharp-eyed woman named Elena Marquez. "The support from these heroes could sway public opinion in your favor, but it's a double-edged sword. The UN won't take this lightly."

Max leaned back in his chair, his hands clasped behind his head. "I know. But if this is what it takes to start a conversation about how heroes should operate, then it's worth it. We can't keep letting bureaucracy get in the way of saving lives."

Kira's fingers tapped rhythmically on the table, her expression pensive. "Max is right. But we need to be strategic. If we're going to push for a global alliance, we need to think about how it'll work. Who's in charge? How do we ensure accountability?"

Elena nodded. "Those are valid concerns. But for now, let's focus on getting you both out of this trial. The international support is a game-changer, but we still have to navigate the legal minefield."

The door opened, and Valkyrie entered, her presence commanding attention. "We've been granted a private meeting with the UN representatives. They're willing to listen, but they're skeptical. They see this as a challenge to their authority."

Max stood, his expression determined. "Then we'll have to make them understand that this isn't about challenging authority—it's about evolving it. The world is changing, and the rules need to change with it."

Kira rose as well, her posture straight and confident. "We'll make them see that heroes aren't a threat to sovereignty—we're a necessary evolution of it."

The group made their way to the UN delegation's office, a sleek, modern space with floor-to-ceiling windows overlooking the city. The representatives—a stern-looking man from the United States, a composed woman from Germany, and a stoic official from Japan—sat behind a long table, their expressions guarded.

Valkyrie took the lead, her voice calm but firm. "We appreciate you hearing us out. Our goal is not to undermine the UN or any nation's sovereignty. It's to create a framework where heroes can act swiftly and effectively when governments cannot."

The American representative, a man named Richard Hayes, leaned forward, his tone skeptical. "And who decides when governments 'cannot' act? You? Max and Kira? This is a dangerous precedent."

Samurai Rising spoke up, his voice steady. "It's not about us deciding. It's about recognizing that there are situations where time is of the essence, and bureaucratic red tape costs lives. We're proposing a council of heroes, one that works in tandem with the UN, not against it."

The German representative, a woman named Dr. Greta Müller, steepled her fingers. "And how would this council be held accountable? What prevents it from becoming a rogue entity?"

Golden Phoenix's voice was smooth, her words carefully chosen. "Accountability would be built into the framework. The council would operate transparently, with regular oversight from the UN and other global bodies. Our goal is to complement existing systems, not replace them."

Carnaval's smile was disarming. "Think of it as a partnership. Heroes bring speed and agility, while governments provide structure and resources. Together, we can achieve more than either could alone."

The Japanese official, a man named Hirokazu Tanaka, leaned back in his chair, his expression unreadable. "This is a significant proposal. It would require a complete rethinking of international relations. Are you prepared for the consequences?"

Max stepped forward, his glowing eyes meeting Tanaka's gaze. "We are. Because the alternative is more lives lost, more villages destroyed, more people suffering while we debate jurisdiction. We can't afford to wait."

Kira stood beside him, her voice soft but unwavering. "We're not asking for permission. We're asking for collaboration. Because at the end of the day, we're all on the same side—the side of protecting people."

The room fell silent, the weight of their words hanging in the air. Hayes exchanged a glance with Müller, then nodded slowly. "This is a lot to consider. We'll take your proposal back to the General Assembly. But know this: if we move forward, it will be with strict conditions. Heroes will not be above the law."

Valkyrie inclined her head. "We wouldn't expect anything less. Our goal is to work within the law, not above it. But sometimes, the law needs to evolve to meet the challenges of the world."

As the meeting adjourned, Max and Kira exchanged a glance, a silent acknowledgment of the ground they had gained. The road ahead would be long and fraught with challenges, but for the first time, it felt like they were building something bigger than themselves.

The trial resumed with a new energy in the courtroom. The international heroes sat in the gallery, their presence a silent reminder of the global implications of the case. Judge Hargrove entered, her expression grave, and took her seat. "This court is back in session. Before we proceed, I want to acknowledge the unprecedented nature of this case. The statements made by the international heroes have raised important questions about the role of superheroes in global affairs. As such, this court will take those statements into consideration in its deliberations."

The gallery erupted in whispers, the tension palpable. Max and Kira exchanged a glance, their hands brushing briefly under the table. They had come this far together, and no matter the outcome, they would face it united.

The prosecution called its final witnesses, government officials who testified to the importance of respecting international sovereignty. The defense countered with experts who spoke to the moral imperative of intervening in humanitarian crises. The arguments were passionate, the stakes higher than ever.

Finally, it was time for closing statements. Max and Kira stood, their voices steady as they addressed the court. Max spoke first, his words filled with conviction. "We didn't act out of defiance or disregard for the law. We acted because we saw a village on the brink of annihilation, and we knew we had the power to stop it. If that makes us criminals, then so be it. But I will never apologize for saving lives."

Kira's voice was soft but resolute. "Heroism isn't about following rules—it's about doing what's right, even when it's hard. We didn't choose this path for glory or recognition. We chose it because someone had to act, and we were the only ones who could."

The courtroom was silent as they finished, the weight of their words hanging in the air. Judge Hargrove rapped her gavel, her expression unreadable. "This court will now recess to deliberate. We will return with a verdict."

As Max and Kira took their seats, the international heroes surrounded them, their support a tangible force. Valkyrie placed a hand on Max's shoulder. "Whatever happens, remember this: you've already changed the world. The conversation has started, and it won't stop here."

Samurai Rising nodded. "You've shown that heroes can stand together, across borders and differences. That's a victory in itself."

The hours that followed were a blur of tension and anticipation. Finally, the courtroom doors opened, and Judge Hargrove re-entered, her expression grim. The gallery fell silent as she spoke.

"After careful deliberation, this court finds Maxwell Johnson and Kira Yamamoto not guilty of violating international law. However, let this serve as a warning: while their actions were justified in this instance, the court will not condone unilateral intervention as a standard practice. The world is watching, and heroes must tread carefully."

The courtroom erupted in a mix of cheers and gasps. Max and Kira exchanged a glance, relief washing over them. They had won, but they knew this was just the beginning.

As they left the courthouse, the international heroes surrounded them, their smiles triumphant. Valkyrie raised a hand, her voice carrying above the crowd. "To Max and Kira—heroes, trailblazers, and friends. Today, we celebrate. But tomorrow, we build."

The group cheered, their voices echoing through the streets. Max and Kira stood at the center, their hands clasped tightly. They had faced the trial together, and now, they would face the future together—a future where heroes were no longer bound by borders, but united by a common purpose.

The rain had stopped, and the sun broke through the clouds, casting a golden glow over the city. It was a new dawn, not just for Max and Kira, but for heroes everywhere. And as they walked away from the courthouse, their capes billowing behind them, they knew that the best was yet to come.

Chapter 7

As Max and Kira soared through the crisp autumn air above New York City, the skyline stretched out beneath them like a glittering tapestry of steel and glass. The wind whipped around them, tugging at Kira's long, raven-black ponytail and ruffling the edges of Max's sleek black and gold suit. The city below was alive, its streets pulsing with the rhythm of a million lives intersecting. For a fleeting moment, the world felt still, suspended in the euphoria of their newfound freedom and the unspoken feelings that had finally been voiced.

Kira turned to Max, her deep brown eyes sparkling with a mix of mischief and tenderness. "How does it feel to be a free man?" she asked, her voice carrying over the rush of the wind.

Max smirked, the weight of their recent trial lifting from his shoulders like a heavy cloak. "Feels damn good," he replied, his golden eyes meeting hers. He paused, his expression softening as he added, "Thanks for having my back, Kira. I couldn't have done it without you."

She shrugged, a warm smile spreading across her face. "Anytime, Max. That's what partners do." Before he could respond, she leaned in, her lips pressing against his in a tender kiss. It was a kiss that spoke of trust, of shared struggles, and of the bond they had forged through trials both literal and metaphorical.

Max pulled back, surprised, his heart racing. "What was that for?" he asked, his voice laced with curiosity.

Kira's smile deepened as she met his gaze. "Because I care about you, Max. A lot."

His chest tightened, emotions swirling as he admitted, "I feel the same. I've wanted this for a while."

She nodded, her eyes shining. "Me too."

Their lips met once more, a fiery collision that ignited the air around them. Kira's hands, calloused from years of swordplay, gripped Max's broad shoulders, her fingers digging into the sleek fabric of his black and gold suit. Max's arms wrapped tightly around her waist, pulling her closer as if to erase any space between them. The kiss was hungry, desperate, a release of pent-up longing that neither had dared to voice. Kira's red and white leotard pressed against his chest, the fabric a stark contrast to his ebony skin, as their bodies moved in sync, their hearts pounding in rhythm.

The wind seemed to hold its breath, as if New York City itself paused to witness their moment. The neon lights of Times Square blurred into a distant glow, the honking horns and bustling crowds fading into silence. Kira's raven-black ponytail brushed against Max's cheek, and he inhaled the faint scent of cherry blossoms that always clung to her hair, a reminder of the quiet moments they rarely shared. His golden eyes, usually alight with nervous energy, softened as he deepened the kiss, his strength tempered by tenderness.

Kira's lips parted slightly, and Max's thumb brushed her jawline, tracing the subtle scar above her left eyebrow—a mark of her battles, a reminder of her strength. She shivered at his touch, not from the chill of the night air but from the warmth of his skin against hers. His invincibility felt like a promise, a shield around them, as if nothing in the world could harm her as long as he held her.

Their kisses slowed, but the intensity remained, every touch and breath charged with unspoken feelings. Kira's fingers tangled in the short afro of his hair, pulling him closer still, as if to imprint this moment into her memory. Max's lips trailed from her mouth to her ear, his breath hot against her skin. "Kira," he whispered, his voice hoarse with emotion, "I—"

But words were unnecessary. The city's energy surged back around them, the world resuming its chaotic rhythm, yet they remained suspended in their own private universe. Kira's brown eyes met his glowing gold ones, and in that gaze, they found everything they needed to say. Their bond, forged in battles and shared silences, deepened with every heartbeat, every touch, every unspoken vow.

And as they pulled apart, the fierceness of their kiss lingered, a silent promise that no matter the challenges ahead, they would face them together.

"I've never felt this way about anyone before. I want to be your boyfriend, Kira."

She pulled back slightly, her smile radiant. "I want that too."

They both giggled, the tension breaking into joyful laughter. "Want to head back to my place?" she suggested, her voice teasing. "Celebrate our new relationship?"

Max grinned, nodding eagerly. "Absolutely."

But as they began to descend toward Kira's loft in Brooklyn, a deafening explosion ripped through the city below. The ground shook, and debris flew into the air, casting a dark plume of smoke against the afternoon sky. The moment of peace they had shared was shattered, replaced by the urgent call of duty.

Max and Kira exchanged a knowing glance, their smiles fading into determined expressions. "Rain check?" Max quipped, a grin tugging at his lips.

Kira nodded, her eyes hardening with resolve. "Let's go kick this supervillain's ass." She giggled, a mix of excitement and adrenaline in her voice.

With a swift motion, she let go of him, free-falling toward the street with effortless grace. Her red and white leotard billowed slightly as she descended, her long skirt with its high slit fluttering behind her like a banner. Max watched her fall, a smile spreading across his face as he realized he was the luckiest superhero on earth. "Come on," he called out, diving after her, ready to face whatever chaos awaited them—together.

The explosion had originated in the heart of Manhattan, near Times Square. As Max and Kira landed on the edge of the chaos, they were greeted by the sight of crumbling buildings, shattered glass, and panicked civilians running in every direction. The air was thick with the smell of smoke and fear.

"Stay back!" Kira shouted, her voice cutting through the noise as she drew her sword, its blade gleaming in the sunlight. She moved with precision, her samurai training evident in every fluid motion as she guided a group of civilians to safety.

Max scanned the area, his golden eyes narrowing as he spotted the source of the destruction. A massive figure, easily thirty feet tall, stood amidst the rubble. It was Tremor, the villain they had faced before, but something was different. His body was now encased in a shimmering, crystalline exoskeleton, and his eyes glowed with an eerie, otherworldly light.

"Looks like our old friend got an upgrade," Max muttered, his fists clenching as he prepared to charge.

"Max, wait!" Kira called out, her voice sharp. "We don't know what he's capable of now. We need to assess the situation first."

Max hesitated, his instincts warring with his desire to protect Kira. "You're right," he conceded, taking a deep breath. "Let's do this smart."

Tremor roared, the sound reverberating through the streets as he slammed a crystalline fist into the ground, sending shockwaves rippling through the pavement. Buildings trembled, and more debris rained down, but Max and Kira were already in motion.

Kira darted forward, her sword slicing through the air with deadly accuracy. She aimed for Tremor's exposed joints, attempting to disable his massive limbs. Max followed, using his super speed to dodge the villain's attacks while delivering blows of his own. His fists connected with Tremor's exoskeleton, but the crystalline material absorbed the impact, barely cracking under the force.

"This isn't working!" Max shouted, his frustration mounting. "We need a new plan!"

Kira nodded, her eyes flicking to a nearby construction site. "Over there!" she yelled, pointing to a crane towering above the chaos. "If we can bring that down on him, it might buy us some time."

Max didn't hesitate. With a burst of speed, he raced toward the crane, using his strength to climb its towering height. Kira followed, her agility allowing her to scale the structure with ease. At the top, they worked together to detach the crane's hook, guiding it to swing toward Tremor.

"Now!" Kira shouted.

Max unleashed a blast of his super strength, sending the crane crashing down onto Tremor. The impact was immense, the exoskeleton cracking under the weight. Tremor roared in pain, staggering backward as the crane collapsed around him.

"That's our chance!" Kira yelled, leaping from the crane's wreckage. She landed gracefully, her sword at the ready as she charged toward Tremor. Max followed, his fists glowing with energy as he prepared to deliver the final blow.

But Tremor wasn't finished. With a surge of power, he shook off the debris, his crystalline form regenerating at an alarming rate. His eyes locked onto Kira, and he lunged, his massive hand swiping toward her.

Max saw the attack coming and acted without thinking. He pushed Kira out of the way, taking the full force of Tremor's blow himself. The impact sent him flying, his body crashing into a nearby building. Pain exploded through his invincible frame, but he forced himself to his feet, his golden eyes blazing with determination.

"Max!" Kira shouted, her voice filled with concern as she rushed to his side. "Are you okay?"

"I'm fine," he grunted, shaking off the dizziness. "But we need to end this now."

Kira's expression hardened. "Then let's do it."

They charged Tremor together, their attacks synchronized and relentless. Kira's sword struck with precision, chipping away at the exoskeleton, while Max's blows shattered the crystalline material piece by piece. Tremor fought back, his attacks growing wilder as his defenses weakened.

Finally, Max saw an opening. With a mighty roar, he unleashed a blast of energy, his fists glowing brighter than ever before. The attack struck Tremor directly, overwhelming his regenerative abilities. The villain let out a final, deafening roar before collapsing into a pile of shattered crystal.

Silence fell over the city, broken only by the distant wail of sirens and the murmurs of relieved civilians. Max and Kira stood side by side, their chests heaving as they caught their breath.

"That was too close," Kira said, her voice trembling slightly as she sheathed her sword.

Max nodded, his eyes scanning the area for any remaining threats. "But we did it. Together."

She turned to him, a small smile playing on her lips. "Together."

For a moment, they simply stood there, the weight of their shared victory settling over them. The city around them was in ruins, but in that instant, it felt like the only thing that mattered was the bond between them.

"So," Max said, breaking the silence with a grin. "About that rain check..."

Kira laughed, a sound that was music to his ears. "I think we've earned it."

Hand in hand, they walked away from the chaos, leaving the cleanup to the authorities and the other heroes who were already arriving on the scene. As they made their way toward Kira's loft, Max couldn't help but feel a sense of peace. The world was far from perfect, and their lives as heroes would always be filled with danger and uncertainty. But with Kira by his side, he knew they could face anything.

The sun was beginning to set as they reached her building, casting a golden glow over the city. Max turned to Kira, his heart full. "Ready to celebrate?" he asked, his voice soft but filled with promise.

She smiled, her eyes meeting his. "Ready."

As they stepped into the elevator, Max pulled her close, their lips meeting in a kiss that spoke of everything they had been through and everything they hoped for. The doors closed, sealing them in their own world, if only for a moment.

Outside, the city continued to heal, its scars a reminder of the battles fought and won. But for Max and Kira, the future was theirs to shape, together. And as the elevator ascended, they knew that no matter what challenges lay ahead, they would face them as partners—in heroism, in love, and in life.

Chapter 8

The moment the loft door clicked shut behind them, the weight of the city's chaos dissolved into the quiet sanctuary of Kira's apartment. The air was thick with the scent of victory and unspoken desire, a heady mix that clung to their skin like a second layer. Max's golden eyes, still glowing faintly from the battle, locked onto Kira's as she turned to face him, her raven-black ponytail swaying like a pendulum of anticipation. Without a word, they began to shed their costumes, the fabric falling away like discarded identities. Kira's red and white leotard slid to the floor, revealing the lean, muscular frame of a woman who had spent her life honing her body into a weapon of precision. Max's black and gold suit followed, pooling around his feet, his chiseled physique a testament to the power that coursed through him.

"Shower," Kira said, her voice low and commanding, as if the word itself were a spell. Max didn't need to be told twice. They moved as one, their footsteps synchronized, the unspoken language of lovers guiding them toward the bathroom. The steam was already rising by the time they stepped in, the hot water cascading over their bodies like a baptism, washing away the grime of battle and the tension of the day. Kira reached for the soap, her hands moving with deliberate slowness as she lathered her palms, the slickness of the suds a stark contrast to the roughness of her calloused skin.

"Come here," she murmured, her eyes never leaving Max's as she stepped closer, her body a tantalizing silhouette through the steam. Max obeyed, his movements deliberate, his gaze devouring her. She pressed her soapy hands to his chest, her touch both gentle and demanding, her fingers tracing the contours of his muscles as if mapping uncharted territory. Max groaned softly, his head tilting back as her hands slid lower, the soap creating a slippery path down his abs, over the ridge of his hips, and—

"Not yet," Kira whispered, her lips brushing against his ear, her breath hot against his skin. She stepped back, her eyes glinting with mischief, and Max's lips curled into a grin. This was Kira—always in control, always pushing the boundaries of what he thought he could handle. He loved it.

The shower became a battlefield of desire, their kisses hungry and desperate, their bodies pressing together, the water pounding down on them like a symphony of pleasure. Kira's hands were everywhere, her touch both tender and rough, her fingers digging into his shoulders as she pulled him closer, her lips trailing down his neck, her teeth grazing his skin in a way that made him shudder. Max responded in kind, his hands roaming over her body, his thumbs brushing the peaks of her breasts, his fingers splaying across her back, pulling her tighter against him. The soap became a weapon of seduction, their bodies sliding against each other, the slickness heightening every sensation.

"Kira," Max gasped, his voice hoarse as she pressed her body against his, her nipples hard against his chest, her core grinding against his erection. She smirked, her eyes dark with desire, and stepped back, turning her back to him. "Wash my back," she commanded, her voice a velvet whip.

Max didn't hesitate. He stepped behind her, his hands gripping her hips as he pressed his chest to her back, his erection throbbing against her ass. He lathered her skin, his touch reverent, his fingers tracing the curve of her spine, the dip of her waist, the swell of her ass. Kira moaned softly, her head tilting back, her hair cascading over her shoulders like a dark waterfall. "Harder," she demanded, and Max complied, his hands tightening on her hips, his touch firm, his thumbs digging into the flesh of her waist.

The shower became a dance, their bodies moving in rhythm, the water pounding down on them like a drumbeat. Kira turned in his arms, her lips crashing against his, her tongue dueling with his, their kisses deep and desperate. She reached down, her hand wrapping around his cock, her grip tight, her thumb brushing the head in a way that made him groan. "Enough," she whispered, her voice thick with desire. "I want you. Now."

They stumbled out of the shower, water dripping from their bodies, their footsteps hurried, their desire too urgent to ignore. The bedroom was a blur of motion, the bed a beacon of promise. Kira pushed Max onto it, her eyes blazing with dominance, her body a vision of raw, unfiltered want. She straddled him, her hands on his chest, her hips grinding against his, her breasts bouncing with the movement. "Touch me," she commanded, her voice a husky whisper.

Max's hands flew to her, his fingers tracing the curves of her body, his touch both gentle and demanding. He cupped her breasts, his thumbs brushing her nipples, his fingers squeezing gently, his mouth following, his lips closing around one peak, his tongue swirling, his teeth grazing. Kira moaned, her head tilting back, her hands tangling in his hair, her hips rocking against his, her core throbbing with need. "More," she gasped, her voice a plea.

Max didn't need to be told twice. He rolled her onto her back, his body pressing her into the mattress, his weight a delicious pressure. He kissed his way down her body, his lips trailing over her neck, her collarbone, her breasts, his tongue dipping into her navel, his hands spreading her legs, his fingers tracing the outline of her core. Kira's breath hitched, her hands gripping the sheets, her body arching off the bed as his mouth closed over her clit, his tongue flicking, his lips sucking, his fingers sliding inside her, his thumb pressing against her G-spot.

"Fuck, Max," she gasped, her voice a raw, desperate sound. "Don't stop. Please."

Max growled, his hands tightening on her hips, his mouth devouring her, his tongue delving deep, his fingers thrusting in time with his movements. Kira's body was a symphony of pleasure, her moans filling the room, her juices flowing freely, her muscles clenching around his fingers. She was close, so close, her body teetering on the edge, her breath coming in short, sharp gasps.

"Max," she whispered, her voice a plea. "I need you. Inside me. Now."

Max didn't hesitate. He surged up, his body hovering over hers, his eyes locked onto hers, his cock throbbing with need. He positioned himself at her entrance, his hands gripping her hips, his gaze intense, his voice a rough whisper. "Ready?"

Kira smirked, her eyes glinting with challenge. "Fuck me," she commanded, her voice a velvet whip.

Max didn't need to be told twice. He thrust into her, his cock sinking deep, his hips snapping forward, his body moving with primal urgency. Kira gasped, her nails digging into his shoulders, her legs wrapping around his waist, her heels digging into his ass, pulling him closer, deeper. The bed creaked beneath them, the frame groaning under the force of their passion, but neither of them cared. This was raw, unfiltered, the kind of sex that left you breathless, the kind of sex that made you feel alive.

Max set a brutal pace, his hips snapping forward, his cock thrusting deep, his body moving with relentless intensity. Kira met him thrust for thrust, her hips rising to meet his, her body a willing participant in this dance of desire. The room was filled with the sounds of their passion—the slap of skin on skin, the creak of the bed, their moans, their gasps, their grunts. The air was thick with the scent of sweat and sex, their bodies glistening, their muscles straining, their desire a tangible thing.

"Harder," Kira gasped, her voice a raw, desperate sound. "Fuck me harder, Max. I need it. I need you."

Max growled, his hands tightening on her hips, his thrusts becoming more urgent, more brutal. The bed began to creak ominously, the frame groaning under the force of their passion, but neither of them cared. This was Kira and Max, their love a force of nature, their desire a wildfire that consumed everything in its path.

And then, with a deafening crack, the bed gave way, the frame splintering, the mattress collapsing, sending them tumbling to the floor in a tangle of limbs and laughter. Kira landed on top of Max, her body pressing him into the hardwood, her hair cascading around her like a dark halo. She looked down at him, her eyes sparkling with mischief, her lips curved into a triumphant smirk. "Well," she said, her voice dripping with teasing, "looks like you broke my bed."

Max chuckled, his hands sliding up her back, his fingers tangling in her hair, pulling her down for a kiss. "Guess I'll have to buy you a new one," he murmured against her lips, his voice thick with promise. "A reinforced metal one. I plan on taking you even harder next time."

Kira laughed, a rich, full sound that made his heart swell. "That," she said, her voice a husky whisper, "is a promise I'm looking forward to you keeping. But next time, at your place. I don't want to be responsible for destroying any more furniture."

Max grinned, his hands sliding down her back, his fingers tracing the curve of her ass, his cock still throbbing inside her. "Deal," he said, his voice a rough whisper. "But first..."

He rolled her onto her back, his body pressing her into the floor, his hips snapping forward, his cock thrusting deep. Kira gasped, her nails digging into his shoulders, her legs wrapping around his waist, her heels digging into his ass, pulling him closer, deeper. The floor was hard, unforgiving, but it only added to the intensity, the raw, primal nature of their desire.

Max set a brutal pace, his hips snapping forward, his cock thrusting deep, his body moving with relentless intensity. Kira met him thrust for thrust, her hips rising to meet his, her body a willing participant in this dance of desire. The room was filled with the sounds of their passion—the slap of skin on skin, their moans, their gasps, their grunts. The air was thick with the scent of sweat and sex, their bodies glistening, their muscles straining, their desire a tangible thing.

"Max," Kira gasped, her voice a raw, desperate sound. "I'm close. So close."

Max growled, his hands tightening on her hips, his thrusts becoming more urgent, more brutal. "Come for me, Kira," he commanded, his voice a velvet whip. "Let me feel you fall apart around my cock."

Kira's body tensed, her muscles clenching, her breath coming in short, sharp gasps. "Fuck, Max," she gasped, her voice a plea. "I'm—"

Her body shattered, her orgasm ripping through her like a tidal wave, her juices flooding around his cock, her muscles clenching around him, milking him, drawing

Max groaned deeply, his body tensing as he reached the edge. His thrusts became erratic, his cock throbbing with an overwhelming need. "Kira," he gasped, his voice raw and desperate. "I'm—"

And then he climaxed, his release powerful and uncontrollable, filling her completely. Kira's arms tightened around him, her breath warm against his neck as she whispered his name, her own body still trembling from her own orgasm moments before.

Afterward, they lay entangled in the broken bed, the creaking frame a testament to their passion. Max pulled Kira close, his fingers tracing lazy patterns on her bare back. She rested her head on his chest, listening to the steady rhythm of his heartbeat. The room was quiet, save for their soft breaths and the distant hum of New York City outside.

Kira smiled, a rare moment of vulnerability softening her stoic features. "This feels right," she murmured, her voice barely above a whisper.

Max kissed the top of her head, his lips lingering. "It does," he agreed, his voice thick with contentment. "Being with you... it's everything I didn't know I needed."

They stayed like that, wrapped in each other's arms, the broken bed beneath them a reminder of the intensity of their connection. For the first time in a long while, both felt a sense of peace, their fears and insecurities momentarily forgotten in the warmth of their new relationship.

Chapter 9

The city below was a tapestry of twinkling lights, a silent witness to the secrets of the night. New York City, with its towering skyscrapers and bustling streets, lay quiet beneath the dark embrace of the sky. High above, where the air was crisp and thin, Max and Kira floated, their bodies suspended in the clouds. The cool night breeze whispered against their skin, a gentle caress that heightened their senses. They had left their costumes—Max's sleek black and gold suit and Kira's form-fitting red and white leotard—tossed carelessly onto the roof of a skyscraper, a silent testament to their impulsive decision. The world below seemed distant, insignificant, as they focused solely on each other.

Kira straddled Max, her hips cradled in his strong hands. Her raven-black hair cascaded over her shoulders, framing her sharp features, while her deep brown eyes locked onto his glowing gold ones. The tension between them was electric, a current that pulsed through their bodies, connecting them in a way that words could never express. Max's muscular frame supported her effortlessly, his hands gripping her hips with a mix of tenderness and possession. The night air was their playground, and they were the only players.

"You're sure about this?" Max asked, his voice low and husky, his breath warm against her neck. His words were laced with a mixture of desire and awe, as if he still couldn't believe they were doing this—floating above the city, about to make love in the clouds.

Kira smirked, her lips curling into a mischievous grin. "Are you doubting my balance, Max?" she teased, her voice steady despite the thrill coursing through her veins. She leaned forward, her breasts brushing against his chest, and whispered, "Or are you scared I'll outlast you?"

Max chuckled, his hands tightening on her hips. "Scared? Me? I'm just making sure you're ready for what's coming." He flexed his fingers, his grip firm but not painful, as if to remind her of his strength. "Because once we start, there's no stopping."

Kira's smirk widened, and she leaned back slightly, her body arching in a way that accentuated her lean, muscular frame. "Then stop talking and show me," she challenged, her voice dripping with confidence. She shifted her weight, her thighs tightening around his waist, and began to move. Slowly at first, her hips rocking in a deliberate rhythm, her body gliding over his. The sensation was intoxicating, the friction between them building with each gentle motion.

Max groaned, his head tilting back as he closed his eyes, savoring the feeling of her body against his. "Fuck, Kira," he muttered, his voice thick with desire. "You're killing me."

She laughed, a soft, sultry sound that sent shivers down his spine. "I'm just getting started," she purred, her movements becoming more urgent, more demanding. Her hands gripped his shoulders, her nails digging into his skin as she increased the pace, her body rising and falling in a primal dance.

The wind whipped around them, tugging at their hair and clothing, but they were oblivious to everything except each other. The city below was a distant memory, its lights a mere backdrop to their passion. Max's hands slid up her back, his fingers tracing the curves of her spine, before cupping her ass and pulling her closer, tighter against him. He could feel her heat, her wetness, and the knowledge sent a surge of desire through him.

"Harder," he growled, his voice rough and demanding. "Ride me, Kira. Show me what you've got."

She obliged, her body moving with a ferocity that matched his own. Her hips snapped against his, her thighs clenching his waist as she bounced on him, her movements wild and uninhibited. Her head fell back, her hair cascading over her shoulders, as she moaned, her voice carrying on the wind. "Like this, Max? Is this what you want?"

"Fuck yes," he groaned, his hands gripping her ass so tightly she could feel his fingerprints. "More. Give me more."

Kira's laughter was breathless, her body glistening with a thin layer of sweat as she moved. "Greedy," she teased, but she didn't slow down. If anything, she went faster, her body a blur of motion as she rode him with abandon. The clouds swirled around them, a chaotic mess that mirrored the storm of sensation building inside them.

Max's eyes opened, his gold gaze burning with intensity as he watched her. "You're fucking incredible," he rasped, his voice hoarse with need. He sat up, his hands moving to her breasts, his thumbs brushing over her nipples, already hard and tight from the cold air and their passion. "So fucking beautiful."

Kira's breath hitched, her body trembling as his touch sent sparks of pleasure through her. "Max," she gasped, her voice a whisper on the wind. "I—I can't—"

"Don't stop," he commanded, his voice firm. "Let go, Kira. Let me feel it."

She cried out, her body arching as she obeyed, her release crashing over her like a wave. Her walls clenched around him, her juices flowing freely as she screamed his name, her voice echoing in the vast expanse of the sky. Max held her tight, his hands gripping her hips as he thrust upward, meeting her movements with his own. His body tensed, his muscles corded as he fought for control, but it was no use. Kira's orgasm triggered his own, and he roared, his release explosive as he filled her, his cum spilling into her in hot, pulsing jets.

For a moment, they were still, their bodies trembling as they rode out the waves of pleasure. The wind carried their moans away, their voices lost in the vastness of the night. Max's hands moved to her face, his thumbs brushing away the sweat from her brow as he looked at her, his expression tender. "You okay?" he asked, his voice soft, concerned.

Kira smiled, her breath still ragged as she nodded. "More than okay," she murmured, her voice thick with satisfaction. She leaned forward, pressing a gentle kiss to his lips, her body still straddling his. "That was... incredible."

Max chuckled, his hands moving to her waist as he pulled her closer, their bodies still joined. "Told you I could keep up," he teased, his voice laced with pride.

She rolled her eyes, but her smile was genuine. "Barely," she shot back, her tone playful. She shifted, her body sliding off his, and they floated side by side, the city below a dazzling spectacle of light and life.

The silence between them was comfortable, a shared understanding that words weren't needed. They had just shared something extraordinary, something that transcended their roles as superheroes, as partners. This was raw, unfiltered, and real.

But as they floated there, the quiet was broken by the distant sound of sirens. The city below was waking up, its rhythm returning to normal. Max's eyes narrowed, his gaze fixed on the lights of a police car racing through the streets. "Looks like our break's over," he said, his voice tinged with regret.

Kira sighed, her expression mirroring his. "Duty calls," she acknowledged, her voice steady. She reached out, her hand brushing his, their fingers intertwining in a silent promise. "We'll finish this later."

Max smiled, his grip tightening on her hand. "Count on it," he vowed, his voice firm. He glanced at the roof where their costumes lay, a reminder of their responsibilities. "Let's get back to work."

With a shared nod, they descended, their bodies moving in sync as they dropped from the clouds, the wind rushing past them as they fell. The city rose to meet them, its chaos and energy enveloping them once more. They landed gracefully on the rooftop, their movements fluid and practiced as they slipped back into their costumes, the fabric sliding over their skin like a second layer of protection.

As they stood side by side, ready to face whatever challenges lay ahead, Kira turned to Max, her expression serious. "You know," she began, her voice low, "this changes things."

Max raised an eyebrow, his gaze curious. "How so?"

She smirked, her eyes sparkling with mischief. "Now I know your secret weakness."

He laughed, a deep, rumbling sound that echoed in the night. "And what's that?"

"Me," she declared, her voice confident, her posture proud. She stepped closer, her hand resting on his chest, her touch light but meaningful. "You can't resist me, Max Johnson. Not now. Not ever."

Max's smile was slow, his eyes never leaving hers. "And why would I want to?" he asked, his voice soft, his tone sincere. He leaned in, his lips brushing hers in a tender kiss, a promise of more to come. "You're my strength, Kira. My everything."

She closed her eyes, savoring his words, his touch. When she pulled back, her expression was soft, her voice barely above a whisper. "Yours," she acknowledged, her hand still on his chest, her thumb brushing over the golden emblem of his suit. "Always."

The sirens grew louder, the city's call to action impossible to ignore. With a shared nod, they took to the skies, their bodies moving as one as they soared into the night, ready to face whatever challenges lay ahead. Their bond was stronger than ever, their love a beacon in the darkness, guiding them through the chaos of their lives.

As they flew, the city spread out below them, its lights a reminder of the lives they protected, the people they saved. But in that moment, it was just them—Max and Kira, two heroes bound by love, by passion, by a connection that transcended words. The night was theirs, and the sky was their playground. Their story was far from over, and as they disappeared into the darkness, the city below slept soundly, unaware of the extraordinary love story unfolding high above its streets.

Chapter 10

The city of New York lay sprawled beneath Max and Kira like a glittering tapestry, its neon veins pulsing with life. The memory of their cloudbound passion still lingered on Max's skin, a ghostly warmth that competed with the cool night air. He couldn't shake the image of Kira, her raven hair cascading like a midnight waterfall, her eyes smoldering with desire as they floated above the world, their bodies entwined in a dance of pure, unadulterated lust. Every touch, every whisper, every gasp of pleasure echoed in his mind, a constant reminder of the intensity of their connection. Even the roar of the city below, the distant wail of sirens, and the hum of traffic couldn't drown out the symphony of their shared ecstasy.

But duty called, as it always did. The city needed its heroes, and Max, ever the responsible nerd-turned-superhero, couldn't ignore the call. He and Kira descended from their ethereal cloud, their costumes materializing around them like second skins. The sleek black and gold of Max's suit contrasted sharply with Kira's red and white leotard, a visual testament to their contrasting personalities, yet their shared purpose united them.

The distress signal came from the financial district, a high-rise building under attack by a group of technologically enhanced mercenaries. Max's golden eyes narrowed as he scanned the scene, his mind already calculating the best approach. Kira, her sword at the ready, landed gracefully beside him, her brown eyes sharp and focused.

"Looks like our date night got interrupted again," she quipped, a hint of amusement flashing in her eyes.

Max chuckled, the sound deep and rumbling. "Seems like the bad guys have a thing for crashing our parties."

They moved as one, a well-oiled machine honed by countless battles. Max's super speed allowed him to disarm a mercenary before the man even realized he was under attack. Kira's sword flashed in the neon lights, slicing through the air with deadly precision, disarming another attacker with a single, graceful movement.

The fight was intense, a chaotic ballet of fists, blades, and glowing energy blasts. Max's invincibility proved invaluable as he absorbed the brunt of the mercenaries' attacks, his body a shield for Kira as she danced through the fray, her movements a lethal blend of agility and power.

But then, in a split second, everything changed. A mercenary, his eyes gleaming with malicious glee, aimed a high-tech energy rifle at a group of civilians cowering behind a overturned car. Kira, without hesitation, threw herself in front of them, her body taking the full force of the blast.

Max's world slowed down. Time seemed to stretch and distort as he watched Kira's body crumple to the ground, her red and white costume torn and smoldering. A primal roar ripped from his throat, a sound born of fear and fury.

The world around him faded into a red haze. Max became a whirlwind of destruction, his powers unleashed with a ferocity that stunned even the hardened mercenaries. He moved with blinding speed, his fists like pistons, his strength unleashed in a torrent of pure, unadorned rage. He didn't fight with strategy anymore; he fought with the raw, animalistic instinct to protect what he loved.

The mercenaries, once confident and cocky, were now terrified. They scattered, fleeing like rats before a predator, their high-tech weapons no match for Max's unbridled power. He didn't stop until every last one of them was either unconscious or begging for mercy.

The battlefield fell silent, the only sound the crackling of dying fires and the heavy panting of Max, his chest heaving as he knelt beside Kira. Her face was pale, her breathing shallow, but she was alive. A wave of relief washed over him, so powerful it threatened to buckle his knees.

He cradled her in his arms, his voice trembling with emotion. "Kira, please... please be okay. I can't lose you. I won't."

Her eyes fluttered open, brown meeting gold in a gaze filled with love and understanding. "Max..." she whispered, her voice weak but steady. "I... I love you too. Always have."

The world around them melted away. The city, the chaos, the fear - all faded into insignificance. There was only Max and Kira, their hearts beating in unison, their souls intertwined. Max leaned down, his lips brushing against hers in a kiss that was both tender and desperate, a kiss that spoke of love, fear, and relief. It was a kiss that promised forever, a kiss that sealed their bond, unbreakable and eternal.

As they held each other close, the weight of the world seemed to lift from their shoulders. The battlefield, still littered with the remnants of the fight, became a backdrop to their private moment, a testament to the strength of their love.

"We'll face whatever comes next," Max murmured against her hair, his voice thick with emotion. "Together."

Kira smiled, a small, weary smile that held a universe of love. "Together," she echoed, her hand tightening on his.

They stayed like that for a long time, lost in each other, the city slowly coming back to life around them. Sirens wailed in the distance, emergency services arriving to tend to the wounded and clean up the mess. But for Max and Kira, the world existed only in the circle of their embrace.

Later, as they stood atop a skyscraper, watching the sunrise paint the city in hues of pink and gold, Kira turned to Max, her eyes shining with unshed tears.

"You know," she said, her voice soft but steady, "I used to think being a hero meant sacrificing everything. Love, happiness, a normal life. But with you, Max, I realize that being a hero doesn't mean giving up on love. It means fighting for it, protecting it, cherishing it."

Max pulled her close, his arms a safe haven around her. "You're my everything, Kira. My partner, my love, my reason for fighting. I'll always protect you, no matter the cost."

They stood there, bathed in the golden light of dawn, their silhouettes etched against the skyline, a symbol of hope, love, and the unyielding power of the human spirit.

The city below bustled with life, its inhabitants unaware of the silent guardians watching over them. But Max and Kira knew their role, their purpose. They were the protectors, the defenders, the embodiment of love and justice in a world that often seemed devoid of both.

And as they soared into the sky, hand in hand, ready to face whatever challenges the future held, they knew one thing with absolute certainty: their love was stronger than any villain, any danger, any obstacle. Their love was their superpower, and together, they were invincible.

Epilogue

Months later, as the city celebrated its annual Hero Appreciation Day, Max and Kira stood on a balcony overlooking the festivities. The streets were filled with cheering crowds, colorful banners fluttering in the breeze, and children dressed as their favorite heroes.

"Quite a change from our first patrol, huh?" Kira remarked, a nostalgic smile playing on her lips.

Max chuckled, his arm tightening around her waist. "Yeah, back then I was just a nervous nerd trying not to trip over my own cape."

"And now you're the city's most beloved hero," Kira said, her eyes sparkling with pride. "Not to mention, the love of my life."

Max pulled her closer, his lips brushing against her ear. "And you're my samurai princess, my partner in crime, my everything."

They shared a kiss, a kiss that silenced the world around them, a kiss that spoke of a love that had weathered storms, battled villains, and emerged stronger than ever.

As the fireworks erupted in the night sky, painting the city in a kaleidoscope of colors, Max and Kira knew that their happily ever after wasn't just a dream. It was their reality, a reality built on love, courage, and the unyielding belief that even in a world of darkness, love could conquer all.

Don't miss out!

Visit the website below and you can sign up to receive emails whenever Matthew Gage publishes a new book. There's no charge and no obligation.

https://books2read.com/r/B-A-QBFOD-VULDG

BOOKS 2 READ

Connecting independent readers to independent writers.

Did you love *The Power Couple*? Then you should read *Love & War: The Battle of Virginia Beach*[1] by Michael Gordon!

[2]

After sleeping in from a steamy one-night stand, Brandon Hill and Hilary Tork are awakened and surprised to see Russia attacking their hometown in Virginia Beach. Now these two unknown lovers are fighting for their lives to make it to safety. Their journey takes them through the Battle of Virginia Beach, and they see the perils of war, while growing closer together. Will they survive the battle together?

---

1. https://books2read.com/u/mlkla9

2. https://books2read.com/u/mlkla9

Also by Matthew Gage

The Power Couple

About the Author

Matthew Gage is a fantasy and Sci-Fi romance author writing about action, adventure and of course romance. He loves watching comic book movies and tv shows, reading comic books, and playing video games if he has time. He also writes interracial contemporary and historical romance under his pen name, Michael Gordon. Check out all of his books under the MG Publishing umbrella!

About the Publisher

MG Books is the publisher of the pen names of Michael Gordon and Matthew Gage. If you are a fan of Sci-Fi and fantasy romance, check out Matthew Gage's books. If you prefer more grounded contemporary romance, check out Michael Gordon's books.